BEASTS ROYAL

The Works of Patrick O'Brian

BEASTS ROYAL

Twelve Tales of Adventure

PATRICK O'BRIAN

HarperCollins*Publishers*

These stories are entirely works of fiction.
The names, characters and incidents portrayed in them are
entirely the work of the author's imagination. Any resemblance to
actual persons, living or dead, events or localities is
entirely coincidental.

HarperCollins*Publishers*
1 London Bridge Street,
London SE1 9GF

www.harpercollins.co.uk

Published by HarperCollins*Publishers* 2015
1

First published in Great Britain by Putnam 1934

Acknowledgement is made to the Oxford University Press for permission to use
'Wang Kahn' and 'The White Cobra', and to the editors of *Chums* and *Greatheart*
respectively for 'Skogula' and 'A Peregrine Falcon'

A catalogue record for this book is available from the British Library

ISBN 978 0 00 811294 3

Set in Spectrum MT Std

Printed and bound in Great Britain by Clays Ltd, St Ives plc

MIX
Paper from
responsible sources
FSC™ C007454

FSC is a non-profit international organisation established to promote the
responsible management of the world's forests. Products carrying the FSC label
are independently certified to assure consumers that they come from forests that
are managed to meet the social, economic and ecological needs
of present and future generations.

Find out more about HarperCollins and the environment at
www.harpercollins.co.uk/green

TO
MY FATHER

Contents

SHARK NO. 206

I

Shark No. 206

Number 206 was a tiger-shark, a long, lean man-eater, the terror of pearl-fishers and coral-divers. When he was very young he had been taken out of the sea in a net by a scientist in the Ichthiological Observatory, and a ring with the inscription T.S. 206 on one side and the observatory's address on the other had been fastened in his gills and he had been entered in the books as shark No. 206.

Since then, however, he had had time to grow into the huge fish that was known as the Devil by the native pearl-divers of the Island of Waitoa in the South Seas.

The lagoon in which the pearl oysters bred was not very well protected by its storm-battered coral reef, and at high tide the sharks could come in with the rollers as they went over the half-submerged reef. The ground sharks and the bottle-nosed sharks could easily be frightened by splashing, or at the worst they could generally be kept off with a long knife, or if that failed they did not usually kill their victim, but only took an arm or a leg. But neither splashing nor a knife could deter a tiger-shark, nor would one ever be contented with an arm and give the wretched man a chance of life; they would take the whole man, leaving only scarlet water behind.

No. 206 was particularly dreaded by the pearl-divers; he would not stop for anything, and always got his man.

He would rise up from the oyster-beds like the shadow of death, and if once he reached his victim the man was dead.

He did not stay in the lagoon of Waitoa, however, as there were many other sharks, and the divers were very cautious.

One day, when a whaler called at Waitoa, 206 followed it as it left, and fed on the scraps which were thrown overboard.

The twenty-foot man-eater was not proud, and he would eat bad salt pork or potato peelings with the humblest dog-fish; he would often eat the humble dog-fish too.

No. 206 was always hungry; he would eat anything, including tin cans; given time he could digest them, and even thrive on them. The only time that his immense appetite was quite sated was when the whaler, which was in luck, caught three great sperm whales. They were towed along by the ship, and 206, in company with a host of other sharks, fed long and full, and the two little pilot fish which guided him to his prey became fat and slow.

The whaler, however, sailed south until she came to the icy Antarctic seas where the great whales bred, and thither the tiger-shark could not follow her, as he was used to the tropical seas in which he had been hatched.

He left the whaler when another ship crossed her path

and followed the new ship, which was a slow, grain-carrying four-masted sailing ship, schooner rigged. She was from Sweden, and her name was the *Björn Anderssen*.

The tiger-shark followed her for many days until it happened that a Friday fell on the thirteenth of the month.

Now as Friday the thirteenth was notoriously a bitterly unlucky day, the wooden-legged sea-cook on board the *Björn* had felt justified in fortifying himself with rum, and he left his galley to go forward to the fo'c'sle, where one of the hands was known to possess a bottle.

Hardly had he left his galley when the *Björn* ran her head into a comber and shipped a green sea; the waist-high wall of water swept the cook overboard.

The watchful pilot fish darted ahead of the shark. Following his two brightly-coloured guides, 206 came upon the unfortunate sea-cook struggling in the water.

The triangular black dorsal fin cut the surface, travelling incredibly fast towards the doomed man; five yards off the fin disappeared, and the shark's white belly flashed in the sun as he turned over to engulf the man.

The cook had seen his death coming for him in the shape of a great fish, and he had fainted before it reached him, so he did not feel the fierce teeth as they sheered through flesh and bone like butter.

It was all over before a boat could be launched, and all that was left to tell of the unfortunate sea-cook was a rapidly dissolving red stain in the sea.

The cook's wooden leg troubled the tiger-shark for some time, but he soon forgot it.

The next day the sailors took a great barbed hook and

bent it to a thin steel cable, and fastening a lump of salt pork to it they threw it overboard.

No. 206 was the only large shark following the *Björn* so they felt fairly sure of hooking the right fish.

The sight of 206 — and, for that matter, of any shark — was not at all good, unlike his nose, which was marvellously keen, and so he always let himself be guided by his pilot fish, who lived with him, sheltering behind his gills in times of trouble.

They had keen sight, and the shark could easily follow their brightly-coloured bodies, although he guided himself towards his prey to a considerable extent by his sharp sense of smell.

When the salt pork was dropped overboard the pilot fish darted forward, leading 206 to the sinking meat.

The sailors could plainly see the pork in the calm, clear water. All at once the tiger-shark glided out from beneath the keel and took the meat. The sailors all pulled on the cable together in order to strike the hook well into the shark's mouth. It lodged firmly between two of his many rows of teeth.

As soon as 206 felt the hook he dived, but the seamen had the cable wound round a winch, and that checked the cable, pulling the shark up short.

No. 206 tugged for some time before he understood that he was held by the cable. Meanwhile the sailors were winding in the line on the winch. For a few moments the shark let himself be dragged upwards, and then the sense of danger penetrated into his bewildered brain.

Instantly he set his great weight against the upward

motion, but still the men gained, drawing the cable in foot by foot, rewinding it on the winch.

No. 206 felt frightened for the first time in his life, and he lashed the water desperately, pulling against the hook. He did not gain, but he stopped the winding of the cable. He could not keep up the tension, however, and slowly the rewinding recommenced.

The bo'sun went below for an axe with which to cut the shark's spine when they had it on deck.

Fighting every inch, the tiger-shark was slowly nearing the surface when he realized that if he did not get off the hook quickly, he would never get off it at all.

The pilot fish were circling distractedly, but they were quite useless now.

Suddenly 206 gave way and shot up to the surface, flying clear of the water in a prodigious leap. He came down with his full weight on the taut cable.

The great jerk unseated the winch, which tore free from the deck and flew over the side, carrying with it three of the men who were holding the cable.

Instantly the bo'sun, who had an axe in his hand, ran to the nearest boat and cut the ropes holding it to the davits.

He and the first mate jumped down into it and reached the men before 206 had finished wondering how he had got free, for the hook was still in his mouth.

The iron winch, sinking rapidly, gave a hard downward pull on the hook, which tore free, taking some teeth with it.

It took the shark some time to realize that he was free of the hook, but when it got through to his confused brain he went back to his old place under the keel of the ship, where his pilot fish rejoined him.

Strangely enough he did not associate the ship with danger, but only salt pork, which he decided never to touch again.

The sailors, when they saw that the shark still followed the ship, took a stouter cable and hook.

The master, however, insisted that the capstan should be used, for although he fully agreed that the cook should be revenged, he hardly liked to account for the loss of another winch to the owners.

On the next day they dropped the pork overboard as before, and the whole crew from the captain down watched it as it sank. No. 206 came from under the keel, but he would not touch the meat.

Even when it was thrown over with the offal from the galley he picked it out and would not touch it. For three days the sailors tried to make him bite, but without success.

He had got it firmly fixed in his head that salt pork was not good for him.

Then one of the ship's three cats died, and the captain had the idea of changing the bait. Accordingly the cat's body was thrown overboard one clear morning.

No. 206 came from beneath the keel and snapped it up without the least suspicion. Instantly the hook struck hard, and the shark knew that he was caught again.

He dived so quickly that the sailors were taken unawares, and let about twenty fathoms of the cable go over without checking it. This gave 206 a good start, and he streaked under the keel, hoping to break the line against it. But it was too stout, and soon he felt the steady pull of the turning capstan. He had got to the other side of the ship, though and with the cable stretched tightly against the keel, the sailors found that they could not haul the strong fish in by hand, so they fitted the spars to the capstan, and, leaning against them, they turned it as if they were raising the anchor.

> Judah! Judah! Idaho!
> Four black ladies all in a row,
> And one come out of Mexico . . .

they sang as they stamped round. The tiger-shark felt the slow, irresistible force, and he was obliged to give way to it.

Inch by inch he was dragged under the keel again and slowly up the other side.

When there were only about two fathoms of water left over his head he tried his spectacular leap again.

Up he shot in a shower of spray, and he gleamed in the tropical sun for a moment, a perfect curve over the blue sea; he came down with a splash that drenched the sailors, but the thick cable and thicker hook held fast, and in another moment he was hauled clear of the water to the tune of the shanty.

He lashed about in a perfect frenzy of rage, and splintered the rail as he came over the side. When they had got him on deck the men hardly knew what to do with the raging devil which they had hauled out of the depths.

The bo'sun with his axe was knocked flying, to land unconscious in the lee-scuppers.

The heavy fish plunged to and fro on the deck, springing about with almost supernatural strength. He scattered the hands, and it looked very much as if he would get over the side again. The captain dived into his cabin, and came out with a rifle in his hands. Taking as careful an aim as he could at the bounding shark, the captain let it have an explosive bullet in the head.

But 206 died hard, and it was not until the fifth bullet had thudded into his furious brain that he lay still.

They cut him open, and retrieved, among other things, the cook's wooden leg, a gold watch, three sovereigns, and the ring numbered T.S. 206, which the captain sent back to the Ichthiological Observatory with an account of its recovery.

A PEREGRINE FALCON

II

A Peregrine Falcon

 A female peregrine falcon surveyed with justifiable pride the two eggs she had just laid. They were a dull reddish brown with beautiful mottling, and as they lay in the untidy, scrappy eyrie they looked very pleasing.

The falcon eyed them approvingly, and then sat down on them and fluffed out her feathers to keep them warm. Her mate the tiercel returned to the nest in the evening; he brought no food as he had not expected the eggs. Having scolded and flapped about a little, the mother gave the eggs into the charge of her husband, and sailed off in search of supper.

She flew out over the Newhaven marshes and saw a heron flapping slowly home; she dropped out of the sky on to the startled bird, who gave a squawk of dismay and sank to the ground.

The peregrine observed the sharp, upturned beak of the heron, and soared up again. She was too hungry to wait and battle, so she mounted higher in wide circles until the marshes appeared as a flat mud-patch below her, and the downs which surrounded them like green hillocks stretching away to the sea in the south and the weald in the north.

On the banks of the Ouse, which meandered through the marshes, her wonderful eyes detected a movement. Folding her wings she dropped like a stone until she was near enough to see a water-rat, who, unaware of his fate, was eating a small beetle.

A shadow glided over him, and he looked up in alarm, but too late, for in a split second he was rushing up into the air in the powerful claws of the bird.

A speck hung high in the air above her claimed the peregrine's attention; she glanced at it with a swift, sideways motion of her head, and recognized another peregrine, a stranger who lived near Pevensey. Higher still than this bird, far out of human sight, soared the stranger's mate.

They both saw her and slanted down out of the sky in huge circles as they manoeuvred for position in the fading light. The first peregrine was anxious, and increased her great speed, flying homewards towards the Newhaven cliffs where her eyrie and eggs were guarded by her mate. Suddenly the Pevensey tiercel stooped, dashing downwards with the rushing sound of a rocket.

She rolled sideways as he approached her, and down he went, spinning a good thousand feet before he could check.

The Newhaven bird had scarcely recovered her balance when the tiercel's mate attacked her from the side, striking heavily above the right wing. A cloud of feathers were scattered, but the falcon's terrible claws failed to grip, and she broke away, wheeling high for another attack.

The Newhaven falcon saw the tiercel coming up again, and with a harsh scream she dropped the water-rat, and circled rapidly higher, receiving the female's second attack with a quick double roll which confused her enemy for the moment, and it gave the harassed bird time to mount higher.

As the other peregrines sheered off, the tiercel dropped down after the water-rat, which he secured before it reached the ground. His mate flew off towards Pevensey, while he circled to gain height. The Newhaven bird did not want to lose the water-rat, and bore down on the tiercel, who fled away towards his mate. They both flew away towards Pevensey, the female circling and covering her mate's retreat.

The Newhaven falcon was feeling too hungry and tired to chase them, so she flew high over the downs to find a rabbit.

She had no luck with the rabbits, however, as they had become extremely wary through years of attacks from owls, peregrines, kestrels, and sparrow-hawks, who were all very fond of rabbit meat.

Sailing over Caburn the peregrine became aware of a pigeon about a quarter of a mile away flying rapidly towards London.

Her hopes rose, and mounting rapidly to a great altitude she exerted every effort, and gradually overtook the pigeon.

The pigeon flew quickly, cleaving the air with the inherent swiftness of generations of pigeons, but the falcon flew quicker, and stooped on the pigeon with enormous speed, coming down squarely on its shoulders, driving her great claws into the soft body.

On returning to the eyrie, the falcon found her mate still on the eggs; she shuffled him off (he was a good three inches shorter) and inspected her eggs closely: they were all right, and she settled down on them for the night. On the next day the tiercel flew from the eyrie early in the morning and returned about noon with a small rabbit, which he gave to his wife. He brought in more food during the day. About four o'clock the tiercel relieved his mate at the eggs; and she stretched her cramped wings, flapping and screaming at the edge of the eyrie.

Far below her on the beach, a man heard her, and looking up he saw the ledge on which the eyrie was built. Having preened herself in the sun the falcon glided off the ledge and flew away to the marshes.

The plovers all fled before she came near, for they had become cautious from long experience.

She flew low over the long grass, and started a jacksnipe, which shot away, corkscrewing and turning in its own inimitable manner. The falcon caught the snipe when it tried to double, and ate it on the ground.

She flew back slowly towards the eyrie. When she came near enough she heard the tiercel shrieking and calling harshly.

Hastening her pace the peregrine approached the nest from the sea. She saw a man taking her eggs.

He was an oölogist, a great enemy of birds, who had seen her stretching her wings earlier in the day.

He had lowered himself over the cliff from a rope tied to a tree, and had fastened a safety line round his waist.

The tiercel had not been able to save the eggs, which

the collector had just put for safety in his mouth. The mother falcon stooped at the man's head with great force, knocking his thick cloth cap off, and wheeling again for another attack.

The man turned pale, he had not thought it serious enough a matter to hire a helper, and he was alone. The tiercel flapped furiously about his head, and the oölogist was too busy keeping the terrible talons from his eyes to climb to safety.

The tiercel drew off for a moment, and the oölogist quickly replaced one egg, thinking to distract the parent's attention, and he started climbing.

He had not hauled himself a dozen feet, however, before the mother, who had mounted to a great height, stooped. The man's hands were holding on to the rope, so she caught him full in the face.

With a shriek he lost his hold and fell, the thin safety rope snapped, and he fell to the rocks below.

The out-going tide washed him out to sea.

SKOGULA

III

Skogula – The Sperm Whale

In the warm seas where squids, octopi, and the like flourish and grow fat, a large school of sperm whales were feeding. Deep down near the sea-bed Skogula, a young bull whale, was pursuing a squid, which, having exhausted all its sepia, was now shooting backwards by means of its long arms, which it used like oars. The whale caught it, and rising to the surface he swallowed it with every sign of enjoyment. He dived again, and swimming along just a few fathoms above the bottom, he looked out for food, but as he was swimming along rather a cold current he could not find any. So after a while he changed his course and swam towards a rocky place where the sea-bed sloped suddenly upwards. Locating an octopus he made for it. His quarry, however, saw him and ejected a black cloud, disappearing into the ripped-up side of a sunken ocean-going tramp lying on the sea-bed under many fathoms of water. The decks harboured hundreds of crabs and shellfish which had come for the dead bodies of the crew years before, and because of the great quantities of crabs, the octopi lived both in and around the ship in great numbers.

As the whale passed a few feet above the deck, looking for the octopus, the skeleton of a man lashed to the wheel shifted in the current, and the skull rolled down the sloping deck, dislodging some crabs who lived inside. As the crabs came out the whale saw the whip-like tentacle of the octopus shoot out after them from the broken window of the charthouse.

The whale swam down and seized the tentacle, hoping to drag the octopus out by it, but the arm snapped off short, so he rose to the surface and spouted several times. He could see the rest of the school of whales lying awash a short distance away.

Just then his mother rose near him, finishing a squid. She was one of the seven wives of the leader of the school. Her husband was a great bull in his prime, fully sixty feet long, who ruled the school with a rod of iron, or rather with his ten-foot ivory-clad under-jaw, with which he had fought his way to the head of the school (in his youth) and had held that position ever since.

Like the other whales, Skogula's mother was looking rather anxious, and he wondered why, for he did not know, as the others did, that his father had decided that the school should migrate farther south.

Skogula's mother was particularly worried, for she knew that he would have to swim with the school for long distances and the pace set by his father, as there were no young calves in the school at the time, would be quite fast. She did not know whether Skogula would be able to stand it.

But he continued ignorant until the next morning, when his father swam right round the school, then he sounded and coming up again at a great pace, he leapt clear of the water and, with a great splash, took up his place at the head of the school and started off southwards.

For a long time they swam steadily, rising to spout every few minutes, until the leader heard, very far off the cry: 'There she blows!' He could not see the ship, being unable to see far in air, but he knew the cry, having been harpooned once. He was very much alarmed, as Skogula could see, and began to take in vast quantities of air, spouting noisily.

The whaler was lowering boats; Skogula could just hear the sound of men rowing them, and a moment later his father dived, showing his great tail for a second before he disappeared; the rest of the school followed him and they all sank to a great depth.

After some time had passed, Skogula felt in need of air, and wondered when his father would go up to the surface. But the leader did not rise, so Skogula left the school, meaning to catch them up later, and rose to the surface.

He emerged near one of the boats, and spouted at once. He did not see the boat as it was behind him. As he was spouting the mate in charge of the boat edged it close enough, and the harpooner seized his first harpoon and stood up in the bows. He was poised for the cast when a clumsy hand at tub oar fouled the whale rope. This spoilt the harpooner's cast, and his iron, which lodged just above Skogula's left fin, had no force in it. Then the whale dived.

The harpooner darted an angry glance at the clumsy hand, and seized the second harpoon, which was lashed to the first by only a short length of rope; he threw it overboard, as the whale was already under the surface.

The second harpoon, however, went skimming along over the water, following Skogula's blind rush, and it foul-hooked a second boat, engaging firmly in its side. The boat swung round, but the barb held fast, so that the first harpoon tore out of Skogula's side.

Meanwhile the school had risen some distance away, and Skogula, when he had calmed down a little, went towards them and found that he had not been missed by the others. Meanwhile the boats were returning to the ship, as a dense fog had risen.

But from that day on, Skogula never trusted boats again. The school only rested for a few hours before the leader ploughed on again, and by nightfall they were a great way from the old feeding grounds. For a long time the whales continued in this way, sometimes passing ships from which their leader always hurried them away at a great pace, and they were never attacked. In time Skogula lost a lot of his extra fat, and drew on his blubber reserves.

At last, after a longer swim than usual, the leader stopped, for Skogula's father knew this place very well, having led the school there more times than he could count, for he had been born there.

Skogula lay awash for some time before he began to look around, as he was very tired. Then he raised himself a little higher out of the water so that he could see that he was in a sort of deep lagoon which was bounded on his left by a crescent of tiny islands. These extended in a serrated half moon to meet another crescent formed of white rock, stretching from a slightly larger island which had a little vegetation.

The islands were too small to support any men or animals other than a few seals, sea-elephants, manatees, and dugongs, who lived on the fish which abounded there.

But birds lived there in thousands; on the main island legions of penguins waddled about, and myriads of gulls dwelt on the smaller rocky islands.

Besides the gulls, there were also frigate birds, boobies, solans, albatrosses, swallow terns, albacores, and many others, including one old fishing eagle, blown there from the north in a great wind.

Skogula found that there was excellent food to be had in the lagoon, where the squids grew to a much larger size than those which he had found in the old feeding ground.

But he was disappointed to find that the octopi were no better than those which he had eaten before, though he was glad to find that there were more of them.

A long time passed while the school lived in the lagoon, feeding well and growing fat and contented.

Skogula was dozing at the surface, digesting an unusually large dinner of squids, one day, when a small school of sperm whales approached the lagoon. They were led by a remarkably large young bull, who made for the main entrance of the lagoon.

Skogula's father saw him and swam out to meet him, circling round in a large sweep; these tactics puzzled the newcomer, who soon laid himself open to a side attack. As he did not turn quickly enough, the older bull charged at once, tearing a piece of blubber from the other's side.

Then Skogula's father dived and attacked the newcomer from the other side. Soon the water around the younger bull grew pink, and sharks approached from all sides. After a little time, however, the newcomer managed to get face to face with his antagonist, and in a moment their great jaws were interlocked. After a while they broke away, and the newcomer managed to get a hold on his enemy's left fin, crushing and crippling it.

Skogula's father creamed the water all round with the lashing of his tail, and then he charged forward again, and the fight continued furiously. After a lot of ineffectual butting, the whales got their jaws interlocked again, and they raged up and down until they passed beyond Skogula's sight; but he could trace their path by the movements of the dense cloud of hoarsely screaming gulls, who followed them, but soon he lost sight of even the gulls, though he could hear the whales beating the water into foam a great way off.

Some time later the younger bull returned alone to the lagoon, though he was badly wounded in a score of places. Skogula never saw his father again. He might have been killed, but that was not likely. He had probably been badly beaten and, if so, he would go away from the school for ever up to the northern seas.

Of course, the victorious survivor took over the command of both schools, which soon merged into one large one, and under his leadership they followed just where his fancy prompted him.

The whales had gone great distances before under their old leader, but now they went even farther afield, never resting in the same place for more than a week. Skogula had fed in the Indian Ocean in one month and off Zanzibar in the next.

But before a great time had passed, Skogula began to notice that the new leader was not nearly so pleasant as his father had been; he was bad tempered and loved to bully the younger whales, who all came to avoid him as much as they could.

Once, as Skogula was pursuing an octopus near St. Helena, the leader snapped it up in front of his nose. This was an insult, but Skogula thought that it would be unwise to attack the aggressor, as he would not have a chance and would only be hurt and driven from the school, so he turned aside to look for another meal.

This occurred again on the next day and the next, until at last Skogula grew quite used to it. A long time passed, during which time the whales had gone a great distance. But as they did not travel in any kind of formation as they did under Skogula's father, some of the smaller cows and calves were eaten by sharks.

Two of the larger bulls who had swum far from the rest were also attacked by giant swordfish, and one was killed. Skogula was once attacked by three of them when he was feeding. They attacked from below, trying to thrust their swords into his soft underparts, and he was forced to leap clear of the water to avoid them.

As he came down, he lashed out furiously, and by a lucky stroke managed to hit one of them on the side of the head with his tail, killing it at once.

Meanwhile the other two were attacking him from the front. One charged at his head, and the other attacked him from the side; the first merely bounced off, but the other buried his sword just above his right fin, and Skogula spouted dark red blood. His temper was now fully aroused, and for the first time, using his full strength, he lashed with his tail hard enough to blind his enemies, and then turning, he bit one right through the middle of the body and the sharks who were waiting all around tore the wounded swordfish into fragments. The survivor was now joined by another swordfish, and they harassed Skogula from behind, but the whale whipped round with astonishing agility. He snapped furiously at them, but missed, and was forced to leap into the air again, for they had got underneath him. On coming down, he dived deep with the fish in full pursuit.

Skogula had taken in enough air to stay down for a long time, so he went very deep, and at last the swordfish gave it up. Skogula was badly hurt, and as he swam back to the school he felt at least three places in his tail where the swords had gone right through. It took him a long time to recover, but when he did, he knew as much about fighting swordfish as any whale, for he had thought out, in a dim way, defensive tactics for the future.

He was able to put the plans into execution before long, as he was attacked by five very large swordfish when some distance south of the Cape. He took his opponents quite by surprise, killed two, and chased the others for a long way.

After his victory over the swordfish Skogula began to realize his strength, and he started to look rather strangely at his leader when that whale took away his food; and his thoughts turned towards the possibilities of challenging the tyrant, defeating him, and taking command over the school.

In his imagination he saw himself the leader of the largest school in the sea, holding undisputed sway over all their doings.

At length the whales began to move eastwards until, after many months, they were lying some distance off the coast of Brazil. On the way they had lost three big bulls and one cow, all four taken by whalers.

By this time Skogula had reached the length of fifty-nine feet, and was still growing, and the leader had long ceased to take away his food.

After a few days the school began to go northward, and soon they encountered a current of water that was nearly fresh; it came from the Amazon, and the whales found it very difficult to swim in.

Skogula thought he must be ill as he lurched and rolled, almost losing control in the unsupporting water. This was not at all to the liking of the leader, who soon turned south again.

During the last few months, Skogula had become increasingly friendly with an attractive young cow called Miska. He had seen her first when looking for cuttlefish, and had felt attracted to her from the first, and she liked him quite well.

When the sea was all phosphorescent, as it often was, they used to chase each other, lobtailing and leaping out of the water as all the whales used to do in pairs, but only at night when the water splashed up like liquid fire.

But as the school was nearing Cape Horn the leader began to take such notice of Miska that Skogula began to feel quite uneasy.

By the time the whales had reached a good feeding-place off the Falkland Islands, all the rest of the school knew that Miska was wavering between Skogula and the leader.

As Skogula did not know half the tricks which whales use when they fight together, he felt a little apprehensive; he also knew that if he put the fight off too long, Miska would get tired of waiting and go over to his rival. So on the next day, when all the whales were at the surface, Skogula summoned up all his courage, and swam across the water to his enemy.

Miska watched him with an anxious yet pleased expression, for she was very gratified at the idea that all the fuss was over her.

Skogula, on nearing the leader, felt fearful, but he put on speed and butted the other in the side. His adversary had been expecting this, and quickly wheeled round to meet Skogula. The other whales retired to a short distance. As the leader came shooting towards him Skogula felt paralysed for a moment, but in an instant he launched out ploughing up big waves on each side as he surged through the water. The whales met with a dull thud, and Skogula saw his enemy half roll over. This was only a trick, but he rushed in to be met by a gleaming row of teeth, which instantly closed on his flanks just below his side fin. Frantic with the pain Skogula tore himself away, and then charged in again snapping furiously.

The whales were enveloped in a flurry of white foam as they raged to and fro, beating up the water with their tails.

The great waves that they made reached an object which was lightly wedged between two rocks. This object floated when a big wave lifted it lightly off the rocks, and it bobbed up and down in the sea.

The fighting whales could hardly be seen for the splashing, but things were not going very well with Skogula, for the blubber was torn from the sides of his head in great strips and he had lost quite a lot of blood. The other had got some nasty furrows down the sides of his head; he was not having things all his own way.

But Skogula was beginning to tire, and it was all he could do to keep face to face with his enemy. The round object was getting nearer and nearer to the whales. Skogula began to attack furiously, for he felt his strength was giving out.

He scored a great slash down his opponent's side, ploughing up the blubber. A moment later they had their jaws interlocked and they tore the water into a thin spume in their fury.

Skogula was half over in the water as his opponent pushed him backwards, when he felt an awful pain and a sharp crack as two of his big teeth gave way and tore out. Suddenly the other broke away and backed for a fresh charge, and though he had suffered rather badly, losing three teeth, he was still much fresher than Skogula.

As the other broke away Skogula had received a terrible wrench which had dislocated his jaw; he snapped feebly and it hurt. The other bull charged, but was met firmly and retreated again. Skogula knew that he could not go on butting to keep the other off, and sooner or later he would have to give way.

His adversary was lobtailing, bringing his great tail down on the water with a sound like that of a gun. Skogula eyed him apprehensively for a moment, when he caught sight of the object which had floated quite near. But he had no time for watching it, for the other was charging with his under-jaw snapping up and down.

The swirl which he made, reaching the ball, brought it right across his path, and the attacking whale bit at it in his anger.

Instantly a great wall of green water shot up with a sky-splitting explosion, and Skogula was rolled over and over by the terrific force of it and felt his jaw slip back into position. A moment later a shower of blood-stained water and blubber and bones rained down from the sky – all that was left of Skogula's enemy – the sixty-four foot sperm whale, after the contact mine had done its work.

PYTHON

IV

Python

In the humid depths of an African jungle the heat of midday struck down on to the tropical foliage and made even the sodden ground steam.

At noon there was not a sound except the monotonous hum of countless insects; all the animals were sleeping. Suddenly a shrill, almost human scream roused the hordes of monkeys which swarmed in those parts. The scream was followed by the querulous chattering of hundreds of the little beasts. One of their number had been caught by a python.

This python was a huge snake, fully thirty feet long, and as thick in the middle as a man's thigh; he would eat anything from a frog to a man, but he preferred monkeys.

Very slowly he would creep up a tree, looking so like a strand of the great parasitical creepers that even the keen-eyed monkeys were deceived, and when he reached a suitable branch he would lie along it and wait for his food to come along.

This python's particular hunting-ground lay along the banks of a swampy river. Here game was plentiful, and the python had lived well for many years. More years, indeed, than he could count, for although he was an intelligent beast, he could not recall happenings which took place before about ten castings of his skin.

His only rivals were leopards, who took monkeys; and the crocodiles in the river, who took the deer when they came down to drink in the evening. The python had long cherished a grievance against one particular leopard, who was constantly poaching on his preserves, and also against one huge, fat old crocodile who lived solitarily in a pool over which hung many trees.

This crocodile, not content with stealing the monkeys who fell into the water when the python had missed them at his first strike, had also snapped up drinking deer from under the python's very nose.

One day, therefore, when he had just finished changing his skin, a painful process, the python, who was feeling discontented, decided to do away with both of his enemies as soon as possible.

He thought that he would deal with the crocodile first, as the leopard generally hunted at night. When he had finished his monkey, which he swallowed whole, the python dropped ten feet of his body on to a branch below. He curled his tail round this lower branch and dropped the rest of his length down to it. This branch led, like a road, to trees which in their turn led to the river.

Thus the great snake went fully half a mile without touching the ground. Throughout his own hunting-ground the python knew similar roads which led to all parts of his domain.

When he reached the river the python drank deeply and had a swim to loosen his new skin, which was rather tight.

He swam very fast, without effort, with about twenty-five feet of his length under the surface, and his head raised above it. He swam down the river to the pool where the crocodile lived. The whole river was inhabited by crocodiles, but none of them cared to touch the python when they saw him swimming past.

When he came near the pool he lowered his body in the water until only his head and a few inches of neck was visible above the surface. But for all that the old crocodile, stretched out on a mudflat near the bank, saw him out of one eye.

The crocodile was a blunt-nosed mugger, a villainous old man eater who was fully the python's equal in years.

Lying on his mudflat with his mouth open and the crocodile-birds hopping in and out of his teeth, the mugger saw the python, but did nothing.

The snake gained the bank and went up an overhanging tree. There he coiled himself in the crotch of the tree and watched the crocodile. They watched one another without winking for more than an hour; the snake because he had no eyelids with which to wink, and the crocodile because he felt the intense animosity of the python, and was too suspicious to lose sight of him for a second.

The day wore on eventlessly, but a little before dusk a baby monkey fell out of a tree next to the python's; it lay on the ground whimpering, but its mother was too terrified to come to it, as she had seen the python move.

As the little monkey hit the ground the mugger slid noiselessly from his mudbank and reached the shore with hardly a ripple to show that he had moved.

For the moment the python had gone right out of his mind, for if there was anything for which the mugger would swim a mile, it was a baby monkey.

The crocodile waddled awkwardly but rapidly up the bank, and snapped up the monkey. On the land he was at a disadvantage; he knew it, and was turning to go when the python dropped on him.

For a moment the snake's great weight crushed the breath out of the mugger, and he did not move.

Instantly the python flung two coils round the crocodile's mouth, and held it closed as in a vice. The crocodile knew that if he did not reach the water before the snake had coiled about his tail and body, he would never survive the fight.

He made a desperate effort, and digging his stout claws into the sand he shuffled towards the river.

But the sand gave way beneath him, and the python had his tail curled round the trunk of a tree, so the mugger did not gain a foot. He lashed furiously with his powerful tail, but the python put a coil round it for all that.

Then the crocodile tried tearing at the snake with his strong claws, but there was not an inch of the python within reach.

He knew then that his only hope was to lie flat against the ground to prevent the python from coiling round his body. Imperceptibly the coils about his head and tail tightened, and the python began to draw him farther up the shore by pulling on the tree round which he had coiled his tail.

The mugger felt himself being dragged backwards, and made a despairing effort. The python's tail lost its hold, and the two plunged into the river, closely intertwined.

By the time they had got to deep water, however, the snake had put three coils about the crocodile's body.

The mugger fought desperately, tearing at the coils with all his strength. But it was of no avail, the coils tightened, his spine broke, and he died.

When he had made sure that the mugger was dead, the python swam to the shore, leaving the body to be eaten by the other crocodiles. On examining his wounds he found that although his new skin was torn in two or three places, the crocodile had not hurt him at all badly.

Towards nightfall he heard a leopard's coughing roar behind him in the forest. He went with his usual unhurried speed towards the noise, and soon he came to a branch on which he picked up the leopard's scent. He knew at once that it was not his enemy who had passed there, but another leopard.

Until moonrise he waited in a tree in which he had often seen the leopard, and a little after the full moon came up he saw him trotting along on the ground between the trees, evidently following some trail.

Very quietly he followed the leopard, gliding from tree to tree more like a wraith than a thirty-foot python.

The scent was strong, and the leopard never hesitated until he came to a clearing. In the middle of the open space a kid was tethered. The leopard sprang noiselessly into a tree; he had not seen the python.

The leopard crept to the end of a branch which overhung

the clearing. The python climbed to a similar branch immediately above the leopard, who was completely absorbed in watching the kid. The great cat crouched flat against the branch; its spotted skin was almost invisible in the moonlight dappled with the shadows of twigs: only the tip of its tail moved, twitching feverishly from side to side.

The python saw the great muscles between the leopard's shoulders swell and tauten as he prepared to spring, and the snake knew that the time had come to strike.

Accordingly he wound five feet of his tail round the branch, and prepared to let the rest of himself drop and coil about the leopard. But the leopard sprang a second before the python had expected, and the snake missed his aim.

The leopard streaked on to the ground and sprang at the kid. Before he reached it, however, he was knocked head over heels backwards, for a rifle bullet hit him as he was in mid-air. A white hunter had tethered the kid there as a trap for the leopard, and he had been waiting since midday in a machan which he had built in a tree close by.

The leopard was killed at once, and after a second shot to make sure, the man came awkwardly down from his tree, for he was cramped by his long vigil.

He carried a revolver in his hand in case the leopard was only shamming. He came just under the tree in which the python had recoiled himself, and having made certain that the leopard had really passed out, he put the revolver back in its holster.

The python liked men; they tasted like fat, soft monkeys. He had already eaten three.

The hunter never had a hint of the python's presence

until he felt a coil round his chest. He made a dash for the open, but the coil tightened, and quickly the python hitched two more round him.

In a second the coils were so tight that the man could not draw breath, let alone call for help; but he still had one arm free, and he plucked furiously at his revolver.

The snake let the rest of his body down to the ground, and tightened the coils a little more. Some ribs gave way and the man felt himself losing consciousness, but he made a prodigious effort, and pulled the revolver clear of its holster. The python threw three more coils round his legs, and tightened them. If he had not been so worn out by his fight with the mugger he would have finished his puny adversary much sooner. He raised his head to the level of the man's face in order to throw a coil round his neck.

This was a fatal mistake; the man raised his revolver with his free arm and blew the python's head off.

There was a pause, then the coils slackened and lost their grip, falling away from the hunter.

The white man blew a whistle for his native servants, who were encamped nearby, and collapsed. They carried him back on a litter, for many of his ribs were broken.

On the next day, being of a frugal turn of mind, he had the python skinned as well as the leopard; the python's skin became handbags, and the leopard's a hearthrug.

THE CONDOR OF
QUETZALCOATL

V

The Condor of Quetzalcoatl

One of the highest passes in the Andes runs past an ancient temple of Quetzalcoatl, a great god of the ancient Aztecs, who is still worshipped by some of the Indians, and this pass is called the Pass of Quetzalcoatl.

For about a mile at its highest point, this pass is a ledge barely a yard wide in places, which runs like a tiny crack across the face of an immense precipice.

The Andes rise above the pass up into the clouds, and the precipice falls sheer away from the ledge down into a valley of pines an incredible distance below.

There was another ridge high above the pass, a small piece of rock jutting out from the face of the precipice. It was entirely inaccessible to anything without wings, and on it there lived an immense condor.

This condor was famous throughout the mountainous country about the pass, and the Indians called him the condor of Quetzalcoatl; he was easily distinguishable from other condors by his enormous wing-spread, which marked him as a giant even among such huge-winged birds as his fellow condors.

The pass of Quetzalcoatl was rarely used since the Spaniards conquered South America, for the gold mines to which it led were hidden so well by the Indians that they have never been found.

About once a month, however, the little Indian village sent a load of moderately rich silver ore south over the pass to Pontrillo, where it was exchanged for the various things that the Indians wanted.

The ore was carried by a train of about a dozen of the sure-footed llamas which the Indians have used since time immemorial as pack animals.

An old Indian called Pepe usually took the llamas over the pass, as he knew it very well. The village also sent him because he had a shrewd eye for a bargain, and would get more value for the silver ore from the merchants of Pontrillo than anyone else.

Now it happened that for about a week before the llama train was due to cross the pass, the condor of Quetzalcoatl had been having very bad hunting. Indeed, he had not had a full meal for some days.

As he wheeled effortlessly thousands of feet above the pass, cutting great circles in the clear air, he noticed Pepe leading the heavily laden llamas.

The Indian saw the condor, and he waved to the bird, for he knew it quite well, having watched it every time he crossed the pass. It gave Pepe a curiously pleasant feeling which was at the same time slightly melancholy, to see the great condor wheeling up on motionless wings into the intense blueness of sky.

As the llamas came to the very narrow part of the ledge which ran under the condor's eyrie, Pepe stopped watching the bird, and concentrated all his attention on getting his heavily laden animals safely across the dangerous part of the pass.

The llamas were loosely roped, head to tail, so that they should keep in a line, but the rope was very thin, so that if one fell the rope would break, and the falling llama would not drag all the others with it.

Just at the very thinnest part of the ledge the rearmost llama slipped, and fell on to its knees, hurting itself quite badly. Its load was too heavy for it to get to its feet again, so Pepe crept back along the edge of the pass, pushing the llamas against the face of the rock to enable himself to get past.

Hung motionless on the wind, the condor's keen eyes marked every detail of the accident.

Pepe was having some difficulty in getting the llama to its feet, and as he pushed between it and the sheer rock, one of its hind feet went over the edge.

The condor turned his head to the earth and shot down a thousand feet, then he steadied himself, and stooped in an immense curve, striking the llama in the middle of the back.

The condor came down at a tremendous speed, but so accurate was his judgment that he shot between the animal and the rock face, passing immediately over Pepe's head.

The llama tottered for a moment, and then fell from the ledge, overbalanced by its heavy load. The thin rope broke with a clear snap. Pepe saw the llama turn several times in the air; it seemed no larger than the palm of his hand when it struck the ground.

The condor dropped after it like a plummet, and Pepe cursed it by all the saints of Christendom and by all the gods of the Inca pantheon. Then he scrambled along the ledge to the head of the train, and led them carefully over the dangerously narrow path.

When they reached the part where the path widened into a safe road, Pepe let them take their own way, and strolled along behind, cursing the condor.

The dead llama had belonged to Pepe; it had been one of the three which he had bought some time ago. The rest of the train belonged to the other villagers.

Pepe arrived in Pontrillo before sunset, but he was distracted by the thought of his loss, and made a very poor bargain with the astute merchants.

He set out before sunrise the next day, for it was a full day's journey home.

The llamas were only lightly laden with the things from the town. They passed under the eyrie at high noon, and Pepe saw the condor sitting there, full gorged and motionless.

He threw a stone at the bird, but the eyrie was far out of reach, so he shook his fist, and cursing the condor, passed on.

The villagers were sympathetic enough not to comment on the very poor bargain Pepe had made with their silver ore, but for several days he was quite morose, brooding over his loss.

In a month's time the llama train set out again; Pepe had

armed himself with a long stick, as there were no firearms in the village.

The condor had been looking out for the llama train for some time, and he followed it at a great height until they came to the dangerous part of the pass, when the bird swung into the wind and hung quite still over the thinnest part of the ledge, watching every movement of the llamas very keenly.

Pepe urged his animals right in against the face of the rock, and walked behind them, watching the condor.

He felt quite sure that the condor would attack the rearmost animal again so he prepared for it, giving the last beast a light burden so that it would not overbalance.

He kept the llamas at a trot so as to get them past the dangerous ledge quickly. He looked at the condor, who was so high that he looked like a floating black feather.

Suddenly the great black bird raised his wings over his head, and dropped; he had seen the foremost llama getting nearer the edge. He checked at a thousand feet above the pass, and paused, judging that there was not quite room to swoop between the llama and the precipice.

Pepe saw what the condor was aiming at, and ran along the ledge to the front of the train.

There was only just room for him to stand on the edge and push the front llama back; this took all his attention.

He heard a rush of wings as the condor stooped on him. He caught a glimpse of broad black pinions, and then he knew that he was falling.

His only feeling was one of intense surprise as he saw the llamas on the pass apparently shooting up into the heavens.

Then he turned in the air and saw the ground rushing up at him incredibly quickly. He had no time to be afraid before he struck it.

The last thing he saw was a huge blue butterfly that flashed past him.

The bewildered llamas made their way back to the village after two days. The villagers, headed by Pepe's son, Iturrioz, set out to look for him. They knew his skeleton by his necklace of red Indian gold; there was nothing else to know him by, for the twenty-three great condors who had followed the condor of Quetzalcoatl had only left the larger bones.

On his father's skull, Iturrioz swore a feud against the gorged bird, who sat on the edge of his eyrie, looking down with glazed eyes, and holding out his wings for the sun's warmth.

Iturrioz went to the ruined temple of Quetzalcoatl and made a sacrifice, spilling blood and salt, for the condor was sacred to the god. Then he went home, and going to his hut he took his bow from beneath the eaves.

Iturrioz was a famous bowman, and he, with two other young men, did all the hunting for the tribe. He took five arrows that had belonged to his grandfather that were only to be used in blood feuds. These arrows were of cunning workmanship; and they were tipped with jasper.

On his thick, powerful bow, Iturrioz put a new string, and then he put the arrow heads to soak in a small pot of cura, a most potent venom.

He set out along the pass early in the morning of the next day. The sun was high by the time he came under the eyrie. The condor was nowhere to be seen.

The Indian squatted down and waited patiently, leaning against the warm rock.

As time wore on and the condor did not come, Iturrioz chewed at a leathery tortilla, still squatting with his great bow across his knees.

He had never seen a firearm of any kind, and, although he had heard of them, he did not really believe in their existence.

At times he thought he saw a speck high in the sky which might have been the bird, but otherwise no living thing stirred. There was no sound of any kind, nor was there any wind.

For some time Iturrioz considered the possibility of reaching the eyrie far above him, but he soon abandoned the thought, for the rock rose sheer; it did not offer the least foothold.

It would also be next to impossible to shoot the condor in its eyrie, for the projection offered a complete shelter from an arrow.

The condor did not return before nightfall, so the Indian left the dangerous part of the pass and went back to a spot where he had left a blanket. He rolled himself in this and slept until daybreak.

At sunrise he rose and went back to the village. There he took a very young llama, which he led along the pass of Quetzalcoatl. The condor was sailing slowly down the gentle wind some way below the pass, but he saw Iturrioz and the llama and wheeled into the wind, climbing rapidly. He soared high above the ledge, and poised himself motionless on his broad wings.

The Indian tied the llama to a long rope, and squatted down on the ledge in the same place as before. The young llama wandered up and down the ledge, for the rope to which it was tied was long enough to let it go a good distance from Iturrioz.

Twice it came so near the edge that the condor started to dive, but each time the bird checked, and each time Iturrioz sank back, releasing his bow with a twang.

The third time, however, the young llama presented a perfect target for the stooping condor.

The bird swooped from its great height; the Indian stood erect, perfectly still, with his arrow drawn to his ear.

The condor grew nearer and larger, and Iturrioz heard the rush of its wings. Then he loosed his arrow, the aim was true, and the jasper-headed arrow passed clean through the bird's body, so strong was the bow.

The condor, jerked out of its course, screamed, and missed the llama. It shot down past the ledge, and then wheeled slowly up, hoping to gain its eyrie.

With lightning rapidity the Indian shot his remaining four arrows into the condor. He shot so quickly and so true that the four shafts were all in the air at one time, and they all found their mark.

The condor almost reached its eyrie before it died in the air. Then it circled down; the huge outspread wings supported the dead bird for a time, but soon it slipped sideways and hurtled down.

A drop of deep red blood fell on the ledge, where it dried quickly in the fierce sun.

OLD CRONK

VI

Old Cronk

A heron was flying slowly over the marshes a little before daybreak. There was light enough to fish by, and the four clamorous youngsters in the nest at home would soon be wanting food.

The country people who lived in and about the marsh knew the heron well, because of his remarkable size and age.

They called him Old Cronk, because of his voice. Landing on the edge of a stream he began walking slowly along the water's edge, peering into the water.

A frog swam jerkily into Cronk's sight, and the heron shot his long beak into the water with lightning speed, spearing the frog through the middle of the back.

Swallowing the frog into his crop, Cronk stalked on. Coming to a little pool, he stopped at a clump of kingcups, and drew up one leg under him, waiting for something to come along.

The white morning mists were melting away as the sun came up before Cronk saw anything. It was an eel, swimming slowly along the bed of the stream with a wriggling, snake-like motion. Cronk's eyes brightened, and he stiffened with a barely perceptible quiver of his crest.

Down shot the spear-sharp beak, and the eel flew up into the air, impaled on the point. With a quick jerk the heron flung it off, catching it again with an open beak.

The eel joined the frog in the heron's crop. Fearing that the disturbance must have startled all the other fish in the stream, the bird waded to the bank, where he gave a little jump, and launched himself into the air, flying with firm, steady wingbeats along the course of the stream until he came to another pool, larger and deeper than the first.

Here he landed on the bank, and waded slowly into the pool until he stood in about a foot of water.

Waiting for the inhabitants of the pool to settle down again after the slight disturbance that he had made, Cronk surveyed the pool. It was about twenty feet across, the stream led into it at one end, and two smaller streams led out at the other.

The heron had not fished in this pool very often, as the water was muddy, and it was not easy to see the fish.

For about half an hour the heron stood on one leg, stock-still, as if in deep meditation.

A roach rose at a fly a little across the pool, and the soft 'plop' that it made sounded clear in the still morning air.

A fat bream rose lazily to the surface near Cronk's feet, and swallowed a little insect that was struggling in the water.

Cronk jerked the bream into the air, and a second later it had joined the frog and the eel in his crop.

The wavelets subsided, and the heron settled down again

to watch. A school of roach entered the pool from one of the smaller streams.

Cronk strode through the water with a purposeful air, making no disturbance. The soft brown mud at the bottom covered his toes as he waded a little deeper. With his long neck outstretched, Cronk waited for the roach to come a little nearer. Slowly the roach came within reach, and the bird raised his head to strike.

Then there was a rush as a great pike shot up from a deep hole, and snapped up one of the little fish.

Cronk had struck at the roach before he had realized the size of his adversary.

His beak had shot in after the roach just half a second before the pike had swallowed, and Cronk saw that he had got more than he could manage.

The pike snapped his strong mouth on Cronk's beak, and pulled. The heron was taken off his guard for the moment, and almost lost his balance, but he flapped wildly with his wings and regained it, jerking twice with his beak to dislodge the pike.

Cronk dropped the roach, and was backing towards the land when the pike, who was in a furious rage, having been hurt by the heron's beak, rushed snapping at his legs.

The heron darted down his beak to defend his legs, and jabbed the fish in the side. Undeterred, the pike seized Cronk's right foot and pulled him over on one side. The heron lost his balance and fell with a squawk and a loud splash, thrashing the water wildly with his wings. Somewhat alarmed by the terrific splashing that the heron made, the pike drew off, watching warily.

Cronk was badly shaken and flustered by falling over, and in his attempts to regain his balance he got out of his depth, and was forced to swim.

He could swim, but he did not like it, especially as he knew that he could not fly until he got to the land.

The pike, a very fierce old fish, weighing between twenty-five and thirty pounds, had lived for many years in the deep hole in the middle of the pool.

He was now thoroughly roused, and wanted to get Cronk over the deep hole in order to be able to drag him down by the foot and drown him. The pike had killed many moorhens and mallard in this way.

Getting between the bird and the bank the pike broke water with a loud splash, hoping to terrify Cronk into swimming deeper. But Cronk was far too stout a bird to be terrified by splashes, and he shot his beak at the pike, catching him, by a lucky chance, in the right eye.

The big fish beat the water into a foam before diving to bury his head in the soft mud.

The heron took advantage of the pause to swim towards the bank. Feeling land beneath his feet, Cronk began wading to the side. He heard the pike shoot clear of the water just behind him. Owing to his eye injury the pike had quite missed Cronk's foot, and he snapped his powerful teeth on empty air.

Wheeling, the heron struck two lightning blows into the great fish, completely transfixing it; he jerked his beak free and reached the bank.

The pike sank writhing, to float up dead a little later on his side.

Cronk shook himself, and hopped into the air, flapping strongly with his broad wings.

He flew slowly, because he was tired, but soon he saw the trees of his ancient heronry coming into sight. He gave a loud 'Cronk! Cronk!' and quickened his pace. A few moments later he landed lightly on the great untidy heap of twigs on which his mate and four young ones awaited breakfast.

GORILLA

VII

Gorilla

Four great apes sat in a tree at noon. They were gorillas, one huge male, his wife, and two small ones. A fifth gorilla, the smallest, was scratching up roots on the ground.

From where he sat, high up on a sort of flat nest or platform of branches and twigs, the big gorilla smelt man. He gave a grunt, and his son on the ground swung up into the tree.

The fierce glare of the noonday sun scarcely penetrated the dense tropical foliage of the forest, and a steamy twilight prevailed except in the occasional clearings.

The largest of the apes had encountered men before, and he had killed two quite easily, but he did not understand them, and so he feared them in a dim, resentful way.

The scent grew weaker, and died away, but none of the gorillas left the trees until well into the afternoon. When they were in the trees they were at home; they swung from branch to branch by their great arms as lightly as gibbons. On the ground they felt lost and out of place. They walked awkwardly on their stumpy bow legs, keeping almost erect by leaning their knuckles on the ground. They shuffled uncomfortably, using their long arms as stilts, when they tried to walk upright; they went faster on all fours.

When it rained, as it often did, they were very miserable if they were on the ground, because they slipped, and stepped in puddles and mud, which they detested, being cleanly creatures. So they always went up to their nest to shelter from the warm downpour, and sometimes they had to sit there for hours, watching the rain. The father had sometimes tried to make a roof to keep the rain from dripping on to him, but he had never quite succeeded.

Sometimes when they were feeding far from their usual haunts they would meet other gorillas, but they avoided them as a rule. Once when they had encountered a solitary, morose old gorilla, he had attacked one of the younger ones, and the big male had gone to his rescue. The two gorillas had faced one another on the ground, half erect, roaring and beating their huge chests. The younger ape had slipped back to his mother.

On that day the two males had contented themselves with roaring, and had not fought, but about a month later the old gorilla had passed under a tree in which his former adversary was hiding. Before he had had time to know what was happening, a great weight had struck him in the back, and fierce teeth had met through his neck, and he was dead. His enemy had remembered, and had hidden on purpose.

The gorillas could talk, although their words were few and difficult to distinguish from grunts. In their guttural, throaty speech the big male was called Urrgh.

Once Urrgh had had three wives, but two had been speared to death when the gorillas had been raiding the sugar canes near a native village. On that occasion Urrgh had killed two men by tearing them to pieces with his hands.

On their platform the gorillas had made heaps of dried fern leaves and grass, from which they made themselves comfortable beds. From the time when he had smelt men until late in the afternoon, Urrgh occupied himself with making a bed.

He selected tufts of soft grass from the main heap and took them to the corner of the nest nearest to the trunk of the enormous tree, then with the greatest care he arranged them to his liking. When he had finished, something in the bed displeased him, so he tore it to pieces, and started again.

Suddenly a change in the wind brought back the smell of man. This, combined with the failure of his bed, annoyed Urrgh, and he got up on his stumpy legs and roared a great deep-throated roar, and thundered on his chest with his clenched fists – the sound was like that of a muffled drum. Then, stopping, he cuffed his wife, and went on with his half-made bed.

His wife, offended, went down to the ground, where her offspring were grubbing up roots.

The veering breeze carried away the smell of men, and the gorilla concentrated on his bed.

Suddenly he saw something glint in the bushes on the ground. He looked down to the little clear space where his family were scuffling about – they had noticed nothing. He looked again, and saw a number of men crouching in the shadow of a thick bush.

He knew that there were more than four, because he could count up to four, but no more.

He was too curious to see what they were doing to give the alarm at once. The thing which he had seen glittering was the barrel of a rifle.

There was a white hunter with five black servants. They were out to catch a young gorilla alive, and they had a net for that purpose.

The wind was blowing into the faces of the hunters, so the gorillas on the ground had no hint of their presence.

One of the smaller apes was gradually nearing the edge of the little clearing; quickly the net shot out and covered him. Instantly Urrgh gave a great bellow of warning and swung down towards the ground. His wife and the other young ones reached the platform as Urrgh reached the ground.

On the ground he paused for a moment, beating his chest. The hunters had all their work cut out to overpower the powerful young gorilla in the net. Suddenly Urrgh charged; scrambling along, now on all fours, now erect, he went faster than a man can run.

The white hunter fired twice; the first bullet missed, but the second struck Urrgh in the shoulder. It did not stop him, however, and before the white man could fire again Urrgh tore the rifle from his grasp, twisted it up like so much rubber tubing, and launched himself at the men.

Two of the natives broke and ran, but the remaining three threw their heavy spears. One only grazed him, but the other two pierced him through the chest. He did not stop for all that, and seized the nearest native in his great arms. He finished the wretched man in a few seconds, but by that time the others had fled, carrying their captive still in the net.

Urrgh dropped the corpse and began to pursue the fugitives. After a moment he stopped, and plucked at the spears. In the heat of the battle he had hardly felt them, but now he felt the pain and roared, pulling at the spears. One came out easily, but the other was barbed, and the head broke off short.

He shambled back to the clearing, where his wife came down to him. She licked his shoulder, and after a few minutes they set off on the trail of the hunters.

They could see the track easily, for the running men had beaten down the undergrowth in their hurry.

The apes swung through the branches after the men, and after a bare minute of hard going they came within sight of them. The hunters were on the bank of a river, just getting into a canoe. They pushed off as the apes came roaring down to the water's edge.

They still had the young gorilla, and the current was far too swift for the apes to cross by swimming.

They returned to the trees, and raced up and down trying to find a place where they could cross. At last they came to two great trees whose branches interlaced over the river. Urrgh and his mate hurled themselves across, and cast about for the trail again. It was some time before they found it, and Urrgh was weakening from loss of blood, but his rage kept him on.

By nightfall the gorillas reached the hunter's camp, which was in a clearing surrounded by large trees. The natives were just beginning to make up the fire for the night, and the white man was standing under one of the trees lighting his pipe.

The young gorilla was in a portable cage. The white man knocked out the dottle of his pipe against his heel, and filled it again.

From a leafy branch just above him a great hairy hand reached down . . . he never uttered a sound when he dropped, because his neck was broken.

The natives saw his death in the twilight, and ran; they would fight in the daylight, but not in the dark.

It was the work of a minute for the two full-grown gorillas to smash the light cage. As night fell the three fled back through the branches to their platform.

In the night Urrgh became feverish, and dreamed of great gestes. He fought with his shadow in the light of the moon, and fell backwards from the platform.

He was dead by the morning.

WANG KAHN

VIII

Wang Kahn

Wang Kahn was chief of all the elephants who were piling teak for the Amalgamated Teak Company. He was a mighty bull in the prime of his life, and he was extraordinarily skilful with the great teak logs that came floating down the river from the forests on their way to the coast and the Company's headquarters.

His mahout, Moti Lal, was the grandson of Wang Kahn's first mahout, and the son of his second. For three generations Moti Lal's family had ridden Wang Kahn, and the great elephant loved his mahout and Little Moti, the mahout's only son; and as they both loved Wang Kahn they were all three very happy.

He was standing in the shade of a tree, with Little Moti between his ponderous feet.

'Lift me up, fat pig,' said the child, and in a moment he was on the elephant's broad back, where he was as much at home as on the ground. Presently Moti Lal came out from his hut, carrying a pot of arrack, a very powerful spirit brewed from rice; Wang Kahn loved arrack, and he came from under the tree with his trunk outstretched.

'Descend, O worthless child, and go and see that no one steals the melons,' cried Moti Lal, giving the elephant the arrack.

Coming down by way of the tail, Little Moti went to guard the ripening melons, and his father mounted the elephant.

He was one of the very few mahouts who never used the ankus, or iron elephant goad, but guided Wang Kahn by speaking to him or by tapping the sides of his head with his feet.

Wang Kahn was very wise, perhaps he was the most wise of all the elephants; at any rate Moti Lal thought so when he saw how he responded to the slightest word or touch.

They went down to the river where the other mahouts had assembled the remaining nine elephants. Moti Lal noticed that the great teak logs were coming down the river in greater numbers than usual, and he shouted across to another mahout, 'Are they sending down an extra consignment?'

'No,' replied the other, 'there was a block up by the Tulwar station, and this is the result.'

Just then a party of men arrived with a fresh load of logs to be floated down to the company's headquarters some 200 miles down the river.

The white superintendent, who rejoiced in the name Smith, rode up on his elephant and gave orders to concentrate on getting the fresh teak into the water.

'But, tuan,' said an aged mahout, 'there will be a jam.'

'Don't answer me, man,' cried Smith, who was young,

and raw, and considered himself above taking advice from a native.

Until noon they worked on the new logs, huge thick trunks twenty feet long, which the elephants handled with a remarkable skill, as they had a perfect sense of balance.

When they knocked off for the siesta (no work was done in the great heat of the noon-day sun) and returned to the elephant lines, the logs were going downstream in perfect order, though rather tightly packed.

When the heat of the day had passed, the elephants were taken into the forest for clearing and hauling new timber down to the river. The elephants all loathed clearing, because they had to grub up roots with their tusks, and scuffle about in harness, dragging great tree-trunks and things.

Moti Lal did not like his son to come down to the river, but he always let him come into the forest on Wang Kahn's back.

They were rooting up a tree stump in a dusty clearing when the alarm siren, the signal of a jam in the river, shrieked from the river bank. Before any order was given Wang Kahn had put Moti Lal on his back and set off for the river.

They found an extraordinary turmoil in the river; on a rock which stood just clear of the water about a quarter of the way across the river there was wedged a great log, and behind it there stretched a mass of logs all heaving and swaying with the force of the stream.

The whole river, from bank to bank, was covered by a wedge-shaped jam, all dependent on the one great log which lay across the stream against the rock; more logs were being brought down every minute, and if the jam were not released very quickly the logs would form themselves into a dam, and flood all the low-lying country round the river for miles.

The river piled up more and more logs behind the block, and Smith strode up and down the bank, very scared, and bawling for Wang Kahn. At last the elephant arrived, and Smith ordered Moti Lal to make him move the big log which was at the apex of the triangular wedge. Slowly the elephant waded in, he had seen at a glance that the thing to do was to give the log a sharp tug to set it afloat again, and then rush back again to the bank before all the timber came rushing down with the terrific force of the pent-up river behind it.

Guiding him carefully through the water, Moti Lal brought Wang Kahn to the log, and they were just about to pull, when Little Moti, who had been forgotten in the turmoil, fell into the river.

The boy could not swim very well, and no one could possibly swim in the welter of rushing logs if once Wang Kahn released them. His father plunged in after Little Moti, shouting to Wang Kahn, 'Hold the logs, *hathi-raj*.' The elephant had heard and understood. Moti Lal had not seen that the great trunk which held the wedge had slipped a little, and was almost free of the rock.

The elephant had felt the log slip a little, and he knew that there was a danger of the whole jam giving way before Moti Lal could reach the bank. He felt the weight increasing enormously as more logs were piled on the back of the wedge, and he knew that if he wanted to reach the bank alive he would have to go at once, and quickly at that.

Little Moti was struggling and frightened, but his father

had got hold of him, and they were slowly nearing the bank.

From the corner of his eye Wang Kahn could see this, and he set his mighty shoulder at the base of the log and pushed with all his great strength. It did not give an inch; things were worse than they had appeared, and the elephant could not hold the mass back for more than a few minutes at the most.

The swimmers had passed out of his sight now, and his only anxiety was that they should be able to gain the bank before he had to let go.

He straddled a little wider, and strove fiercely against the shifting logs whose weight was slowly pushing him back; grunting and exhausted, he made a great effort, and gained an inch. Just then Moti Lal crawled out on to the wet mud of the river bank, and shouted to Wang Kahn, who heard, and trumpeted as he went down in the maelstrom of crashing logs.

His body was washed ashore next day, far down the river, almost unrecognizable.

RHINO

IX

Rhino

A rhinoceros was resting beneath a tree. The blazing African sun was beginning to go down in the west, but the heat was still at its worst, and the dusty plain, sparsely covered with scrub and small trees, shimmered in the heat-haze.

On the rhino's back a dozen small birds hopped to and fro. They were the only living things whose presence the rhino could tolerate, for he was constitutionally ill-tempered; but he liked the birds because they kept away the big stinging flies, and, better still, they removed the boring parasites who burrowed into his thick, tough hide, and made his life miserable.

The sight of any other creature except these birds filled him with unreasoning annoyance, and if it stayed near him his annoyance would turn into rage, and he would charge it even if it were a lion.

His sight was very poor, but his acute sense of smell made up for that. His short sight made him suspicious of everything which he saw moving, and sometimes he would root up a bush that had been moving in the wind on the off chance that it might be some animal.

He was afraid of nothing on earth, but there was not an animal in the bush who would care to try its chances against him.

When he came down to the water-hole in the middle of the plain everything made way for him, from the lions downwards.

Once a lion had tried conclusions with him; it had not lived to tell the tale.

The rhino was a terrible fighter; his immense weight, his remarkable speed when he charged, and above all the single long horn on the top of his snout, combined to make him almost invincible. Once he had got his ponderous body under way his great weight gave him an unbelievable velocity, and at the height of his charge the rhino could outpace a galloping horse.

The pride of his life was his horn. The long, sharp, tapering projection curved slightly backwards; it was unrivalled as an instrument for ripping up his opponents.

He spent a great deal of time in stropping it against the trunk of the same tree against which he rubbed himself, with the result that all the bark of the tree near the ground disappeared.

In much the same manner as a bird whets its beak on a twig, the rhinoceros sharpened his horn against the tree, keeping it sharp for any emergency.

His greatest strength lay in his shoulders, so when he threw up his head the force of the jerk was so great that anything that he had impaled on his horn was thrown high over his back. He kept himself practised at this by grubbing up bushes and small trees, so that the part of the bush in which he lived was freely dotted with dead, dry trunks and branches; it also helped to work off his ill temper.

His only rival in the bush was another rhinoceros, who lived some way to the north, and who was the only animal who had ever beaten him. This was in a fight for a remarkably well-made female rhino.

He had not been quite at his prime at the time when he was beaten, but the defeat had preyed on his mind, making him more than usually morose.

A strong north wind had been blowing all day, but as the sun's heat grew less, it dropped, and a little before sunset a light south-west breeze blew across the plain.

The breeze carried with it a smell which puzzled the rhino. He sniffed the wind meditatively; he could distinguish the scent of the mixed herd of wildebeest and zebra which wandered habitually in the south of his part of the world in that season; that was the prevailing scent, but there was also the musty, somewhat fetid odour of a lion, probably attended by a few jackals and hyenas; it was none of these smells, however, that disquieted the rhino, for he was quite used to them, and knew what they were; it was another smell which he did not know that puzzled him.

It was vaguely like that of another rhinoceros but it was subtly different; it was obviously not that of any carnivore or else it would have had that slightly musty savour that the meat-eating animals always carry about with them.

The rhinoceros decided to investigate the scent, and he went up the wind with his usual surprisingly nimble trot.

Everything got out of his way, for his anger was not lightly to be incurred.

He came to a belt of trees and paused, for the light breeze had failed. In some thick grass nearby he picked up the trail again, for the tall grass held the scent very well, so that he could follow it without lowering his head.

It was evident that about a dozen of the animals had passed there, and that they were not far away, for the scent was very fresh.

Suddenly he came out of the trees, and there, showing plainly against the skyline, were eight elephants.

They were looking straight at the rhinoceros, for they had heard him coming through the trees. There were two bull elephants, one very old, and the other in his prime; they were accompanied by two cows with two half grown, and two very young calves. The rhino's first feeling was one of intense surprise and curiosity; then almost immediately he felt annoyed that these animals should be in his part of the bush.

This annoyance turned into rage as he began to scratch the ground with his forefeet. The rims of his little eyes grew red, and he twitched his ears to and fro.

Seven of the elephants faded silently into the trees, and the big bull remained in front of the rhino, about a hundred yards away from him.

The elephant's colossal ears were outspread, and he held his trunk stiffly out in the air, sniffing. His great tusks shone in the golden sunlight.

The elephant's eyes were no better than the rhino's, but in the clear light of the setting sun they could see one another plainly.

The rhinoceros flicked his little pig-like tail about for a moment, and then, tightly curling it over his back, he lowered his head and charged with a high pitched squeal like the whistle of a train.

The earth shook as he thundered towards the elephant, who coiled back his trunk and bent his forelegs somewhat to prevent the rhino from dashing beneath him, and disembowelling him with a sweep of his horn. The rhino came down on the elephant in a cloud of dust; the elephant turned his great shoulder to take the shock and to avoid the rhino's horn.

They met with a dull thud; a cloud of dust flew up, and the rhino, deflected from his course by the elephant's movement, careered on into a sapling, which he crushed flat.

He had not expected the elephant to withstand his charge, but it did not dismay him at all. He turned, and charged again.

They met shoulder to shoulder again, and this time the elephant slid back a little at the impact.

The elephant could not receive the charging rhino on his tusks, as the great speed and weight might snap them, for they were very long compared with the rhino's horn.

At the third charge the rhino scored a long gash down the elephant's side, and he turned quickly to follow up this advantage, but the elephant had turned more quickly, and bore down on the standing rhino, trumpeting shrilly.

The rhinoceros staggered at the shock, and nearly fell, and before he could recover the elephant gored him furiously. Both tusks pierced him, but neither found a vital spot;

before the elephant could press his advantage, the rhino ran in under the scarlet tusks.

The elephant slipped, and fell squarely on top of the rhino, knocking all the breath out of his body, and not leaving him any room to use his horn. Before the rhino could get breath to rise the elephant scrambled off him and, kneeling, struck in with his tusks.

Fortunately for the rhinoceros one tusk glanced off his tough hide, and the other missed him altogether, ploughing up the hard earth about an inch from his head.

Regaining his feet, the rhino backed away; and the two great beasts stood glaring at one another.

The sun set with the suddenness peculiar to tropical lands, and in the afterglow the rhinoceros circled round the elephant, seeking a good place from which to charge.

With their weak eyes both of them were having difficulty now in seeing one another clearly.

Finding a sandy hillock, the rhino lowered his head and charged. The elephant was standing in the shadow of a tall bush; the charging rhinoceros could hardly distinguish between elephant and shade, so his earth-shaking charge missed the greater part of its effect, as he struck the elephant a glancing blow. His great pace prevented him from pulling up, and he went crashing away into a thicket of thorn bushes.

He pulled himself out, grunting, and galloped back. The elephant had disappeared. In the gathering shadows the elephants had noiselessly slipped away into the trees; the rhino had not heard them go, for with their soft, padded feet, the great brutes could move like shadows.

The strengthening wind kept the scent of their retreat from the rhinoceros, who stood bewildered in the shadow where the elephant had stood, and where his own blood marked the place of the fight.

He peered into the dusk, but saw nothing. Then with a grunt he swung round and made for the dense mass of thorn bushes in which he slept.

He felt quite happy, for his wounds were not very serious, and they hardly troubled him; he thought in his own vague way that he had kept his part of the bush against the invaders. The fight had worked off all his moroseness; he was thoroughly satisfied with himself.

As he went, everything, from the prowling lions downwards, made way for him. Tomorrow, he thought, he would show that other rhinoceros in the north what fighting really meant.

THE WHITE COBRA

X

The White Cobra

A pipal-tree grew in the open space about which the houses of the village of Kurasai were built. It was in the hollow roots of this tree that a cobra had his dwelling.

Every evening, when the people of the village assembled in the open space to talk, the elders set a dish of warm milk at the roots of the tree for the cobra to drink.

In many of the villages of the Punjab there are such cobras, but this one was peculiar in that it was white, with curious markings. It had first been seen on the eve of the feast of Krishna, so it was called Vakrishna, and it was looked upon as a possible incarnation of the god.

The inhabitants of Kurasai were Hindus, but they were tolerant people, and therefore they welcomed a Mohammedan snake-charmer, who turned up one evening, and said that he had come from Peshawar on a journey south. The fact was that Hussein – for such was his name – had heard of the white cobra, whose fame had spread, when he was performing with his snakes at a feast given by a petty

rajah some forty miles south in Fakirpur, and, on hearing
of it, had instantly desired it.

On the same evening that he arrived he came to give an
account of himself to the headman in the open space, which
was also the court of justice for that village.

Slowly he led the conversation round to cobras, of which,
he said, he was inordinately fond. Now it happened that at
this time the headman's youngest son came with the warm
milk for Vakrishna, but the snake would not come out on
account of the stranger.

The headman was chary of speech concerning the white
cobra, towards which he bore himself reverently, being a
Hindu, so Hussein did not press the matter, but announced
that he would be staying for a few days to rest for his
journey.

The headman would only say that the cobra had brought
the village good luck for some years, and the village priest
bore him out in this, pointing out that the crops in Kurasai
were better than those of any village for miles around. 'Not
that we are at all wealthy,' he said hastily, as he saw Hussein
listening attentively, 'but we manage with economies.'
Then he turned the talk to more general matters, and the
priest, eager to show the villagers the depth of his learning,
questioned Hussein on certain points of the faith of Islam.

It transpired that Hussein was a Sufi — a freethinker, as
opposed to the orthodox Shiahs. This at once raised him
in the estimation of the villagers, whose neighbours towards
the north were strict Shiahs, and great cattle thieves.

On the next day Hussein did not speak of snakes at all, but
discussed the Government; he agreed with the headman in

condemning it, and so, by the next day, he felt sufficiently confident to speak freely about the white cobra.

He learnt that it was at least a hundred feet long, and that it spoke with the voice of trumpeting elephants; but it was plain that the simple villagers wished to impress him, so he was suitably impressed. At fifty miles he had heard of Vakrishna as a great snake which was longer than five large pythons, and as impalpable as the mist; by twenty-five miles the cobra had shrunk to a snake as long as three pythons, which habitually ate tigers; and at ten miles it was only a great snake which could kill an elephant. Yet all these reports contained the same assertion that the cobra was white, so Hussein bided his time.

That evening, when the warm milk had been set down in front of the little hole from which the snake used to come Hussein offered to give a free performance with his snakes.

He set down the basket with the snakes in it and squatted before it; the villagers sat round in a ring.

The Mohammedan blew a thin, squeaky tune on a kind of globular flute, and presently the lid of the basket began to rise. It fell off sideways, and a cobra's head appeared in the opening. The tune grew faster, and the snake shot up a foot or so, swaying in time with the tune.

Soon two other snakes appeared, and they crept out of the basket on to the ground. The crowd was quite silent, and the only sound that was to be heard was the shrill piping of the snake-charmer.

The three cobras shuffled vaguely, half coiled, with their heads about a foot from the ground.

Suddenly the tune changed, and the snakes began to

dance. They traced strange patterns on the dust, weaving their heads to and fro, moving incessantly.

Hussein heard the faint hiss that he had been expecting, and turning ever so slightly he saw half the length of Vakrishna protruding from the roots of the pipal-tree.

The hood on the cobra's neck was half open, and its curious markings showed distinctly on the strangely white skin. Hussein caught his breath, for he saw at once that it was the real thing, that great rarity, a truly white cobra.

Slowly he let the music die down; he had seen all that he wished.

As the music became fainter and more slow the snakes danced less swiftly, and at length they sank to the ground. Quickly Hussein picked them up by the neck and thrust them back into the basket.

All that night the snake-charmer lay awake, thinking of the white cobra. He knew that if he took it away he would not get twenty miles, for there was no railway, and the hue and cry which the villagers would certainly raise would catch him before he could dispose of his treasure. By daybreak, however, he had thought out a scheme. He had noticed that they were repainting the dak-bungalow with white paint. At noon he went there and took a little pannikin full of the white paint, and during the siesta, when everyone else was asleep, he took one of his own snakes and painted it white.

It was very difficult to keep the snake still, but Hussein was safe enough, as the cobra's fangs had been drawn long ago. At last the snake was fairly white all over, and nearly dry, but it was in a furious temper, and although Hussein had drugged it before starting, he was hard put to it to control it by the time that he came to try to paint Vakrishna's markings on it.

At length the task was completed, however, and the finished product might easily have been taken for Vakrishna in the dusk. In the night when the rest of the village was asleep, the snake-charmer crept to the pipal-tree, and squatting by the hole he played certain tunes on his pipe very softly. It was a long time before the snake took any notice, but by the time the moon had risen, Hussein heard the dry rustling sound that a snake makes when it moves, and he saw the cobra's eyes gleaming in the entrance to the hole. In the moonlight the white snake was almost invisible, but Hussein could see its shadow quite clearly.

Very slowly Vakrishna slid out into the open.

From beneath his loose cloak Hussein took the body of a young rat; he laid it on the ground and shuffled backwards into the deep purple shadow of the pipal-tree.

The cobra's head glided towards the rat, and then, with an incredibly swift movement, Vakrishna snapped it up and swallowed it. Hussein could see all this by the light of the full moon, he could even see the rat going down the snake's body, and he went back to bed well satisfied.

In the rat's body the snake-charmer had put a certain drug, because he could not handle the cobra while it was conscious, as its fangs had not been drawn, and it did not know him.

By the next day the painted snake became more furious than ever, as the paint made it extremely uncomfortable.

Hussein knew that the drug would act at about noon,

so he made his plans for departure, telling the headman that he would be continuing his journey in the afternoon, when the heat of the sun had died down. So far his plan had worked perfectly, and the only thing that worried Hussein was the behaviour of the painted snake, which was ominously calm.

When the great heat of the noonday sun had driven all the villagers to shelter, the snake-charmer went to Vakrishna's tree with a hooked stick. Quickly he drew the limp, unconscious snake out, and put it into a sack, from which he took the substitute, and put its nose to the hole in the tree.

The painted snake seemed disinclined to go in, so Hussein trod on its tail; it disappeared into the pipal-tree.

Hussein strolled back to his room by a devious way. No one had seen him. He gloated for a while over the white cobra, and then put it into a special basket by itself.

He packed up his belongings and set out, passing by the pipal-tree, where he could see the painted snake's head at the entrance to the hole. He tapped it on the nose, and it shot back into the hollow roots.

He had gone some ten miles by nightfall, and he slept in a village with one arm round Vakrishna's basket.

Towards morning he was awakened by the headman of Kurasai, who was bawling in his ear and beating him with a stick.

They all set on him, and dragging him into the road they beat him until he was unconscious. They also broke his baskets, releasing his trained snakes, and they took away Vakrishna.

The priest, apparently more compassionate than the rest, stayed to revive him, and when he came to his senses, Hussein asked him how they had found out.

'A little before sundown,' said the Brahmin, 'when all the village was assembled, your snake came out, and before our eyes he cast his skin, and I, picking it up in its entirety, clearly perceived the fraud, as the paint flaked off.' And with this the compassionate man beat Hussein more grievously than the others, leaving him for dead.

JEHANGIR BAHADUR

XI

Jehangir Bahadur

Although Hussein was by profession a snake-charmer, he had been born a mahout, and until he had made things too hot for himself in the Public Works Department he had worked with the elephants which his father had ridden before him.

Hussein, after an extremely varied career, decided to settle down on the land and end his life in peace. He had neither land nor money, but, as he said, even the eagle is born without feathers.

While he was travelling about the Punjab with his snakes he encountered a regiment going north up the Grand Trunk Road with all its guns and impedimenta. Hussein followed the soldiers among the camp sutlers, and when they encamped he prepared his snakes for a performance.

Nevertheless, until they had fed he did not approach, for there is a native proverb which says 'Never speak to a white man until he is fed.' After their meal, however, the soldiers were disposed to be amused, and Hussein gave his performance in an open space before the tents.

Soon after the sun set, and the snake-charmer wandered away to the native lines to look for a bed. He learnt that there was straw to be had for two pice in the elephant lines, and he went towards the place where about twenty elephants were tethered for the night. There he encountered the chief of the mahouts, who gave him straw for a bed.

When he had secured his bed with a piece of rope he turned to go, but the chief of the mahouts cried out, saying, 'The price, O son of Eblis!'

'Old man,' replied Hussein, 'who gave thee leave to sell the Government's straw, expressly purchased for the greater comfort of my lords the elephants?' and with this he went away, bearing his straw to a secluded spot towards the end of the lines.

'Now,' said the chief of the mahouts, 'I clearly perceive that that man is fundamentally evil, and that this is an unfortunate day for me.' But he did not pursue Hussein, for he was an old man and disliked tumult.

Hussein made a kind of nest in his straw and burrowed into it. He slept soundly until a little before dawn, when one of the elephants who had slipped his picket ropes woke him by taking the greater portion of his straw.

Hussein sprang up, abusing the elephant in the tongue of the mahouts. It drew back, ashamed; for an elephant is most sensitive to abuse in language which it understands, but none outside the mahout caste understands the peculiar *hathi*-tongue in which elephants should be admonished and rebuked.

The elephant became ashamed of itself, and shuffled backwards into the shadows. It was a bull elephant, with tusks ringed with silver bands that gleamed in the half light.

Hussein went back to his bed, but there was not enough to sleep in, so he gathered up his basket of snakes and went over to a fire which some of the early rising camp followers had kindled.

From one he borrowed some cold boiled rice wherewith he broke his fast. The man who yielded up his rice was a Jat, a farmer from the rich corn lands some way farther north, who had come into the camp to sell fowls. He was a simple man, and Hussein borrowed a rupee from him.

After his meal Hussein went back to the elephant lines to look at the elephants, for his breeding had given him a true appreciation of the great beasts. On the way he came across a man selling sugar cane, and he bought several of the sweet, juicy sticks.

He came to the elephant lines, and almost at once he recognized the one who had eaten his bed by the silver rings about his tusks. The elephant knew him at once, and looked sheepish; then it reached out its trunk and touched him on the arm, and Hussein knew that he had known this elephant long ago.

He thought for a moment, and then it came back to him in a flash; it was Jehangir Bahadur, who had come to his father for training when Hussein was a youth. He had been very fond of Jehangir for the five years that he had known him, although he was naturally most attached to Muhammed Akbar, the elephant which his grandfather, his father, and himself had served — indeed Hussein had not left the service until Muhammed Akbar died.

Jehangir had recognized him as soon as he had seen him

in the full light, and he gave a little gurgle of delight, bending his fore-legs until his head was almost on the ground, with his trunk curled back over his forehead.

When they had stroked and patted one another, Hussein sat between Jehangir's front feet and fed him with the sugar canes in the shade of his flapping ears.

Presently a man came along the lines, and seeing Hussein he cried, 'Man, stand afar off, for this is a lordly elephant, and one who is by no means to be fed by lowly people.' And Hussein answered, saying, 'O *bahinchute*, since when have the drovers of beasts called themselves mahouts?' for he saw by the man's caste mark that he was no mahout, but a mere herder of cattle.

'Nevertheless,' replied the man, somewhat abashed, 'I am the temporary attendant of the mighty one.'

'Has he then no regular mahout?' asked Hussein.

'No, for he will suffer none to remain with him for more than a few months. It is said that he seeks a previous mahout, and will never be satisfied until he finds him.'

'These are true words,' replied Hussein, 'you may fetch me water, a brush, and some arrack. This is an honour, for I am he whom Jehangir Bahadur has waited. On your head and heart.' Now the man was taken aback by Hussein's air of authority, and straightway he went to fetch that which was commanded. The water and the stiff brush having been brought, and the arrack having been set aside in a pot, Hussein washed Jehangir all over very carefully, cleaning his great ears tenderly, and plucking the small stones and thorns from his feet.

When he had done he gave Jehangir the arrack to drink;

by this time several other mahouts had come, and they said, 'Who is this?' They learnt that Hussein was Jehangir's first mahout, and they said, 'These things are as they should be.' For they had spent their lives among the elephants, and they understood them.

One asked Hussein why he did not rejoin the service, and he replied that he had left it quickly for certain imperative reasons, and that he would find it hard to get back again.

'But this is an exceptional case,' said an old mahout, 'and Jehangir will undoubtedly pine if you leave him again. I will speak to the chief of the mahouts myself.'

And all the mahouts said, 'This is just.'

But when the chief was brought he looked sourly upon Hussein, for he recognized in him the man who had tricked him out of two pice the evening before, and he said, 'Now this is without doubt an evil man, a *bût-parast,* and one whose female relations have no noses; who is he to consort with us?'

'But Jehangir will perish if he goes,' said one of the mahouts.

'That is not so,' replied the old man, 'for I shall make him my own especial charge.' And with this he caused Hussein to be ejected from the camp.

Jehangir could not help him, as he was shackled with chains to prevent him from wandering again, but as Hussein was hustled away the elephant trumpeted and raged.

Hussein dared not return to the camp on account of the enmity of the old man, but in a week, when the regiment moved north again, he followed it, and saw Jehangir pulling the guns with the other elephants. He was very troublesome, however, and constantly stopped among crowds to look for Hussein.

The chief of the mahouts rode him, and wielded the iron ankus unmercifully, so that Hussein, watching from afar, raged furiously.

When it came to the place appointed, the regiment was split up, certain of the elephants being sent north with the guns, and the others being returned to south with various burdens.

Among those who were sent back was Jehangir, for it was feared that he would go *musth* and run amok.

The chief of the mahouts went north with the other elephants where he was killed by reason of a stone that fell on his head as he passed beneath a bridge; so Hussein was able to see more of Jehangir. He followed the returning detachment, giving performances with his snakes whenever he could.

In a few days he approached the man who commanded the mahouts, and asked to be taken on, but the man refused, saying that he had been warned against Hussein as a wicked man who sought an opportunity to do evil.

Hussein had no money wherewith to bribe the man, so he cried out to heaven that this was an injustice, hoping to catch the ear of a white man, but the other man shouted louder, and men came running who beat Hussein with their *lathis*, and throwing him into a dry ditch forbade him to come near the elephants again. That night he stole to the lines and lay at the feet of Jehangir; the elephant lifted him up on to his back, and Hussein whispered his troubles into the broad waving ears.

When he slept from weariness, stretched on the elephant's back, Jehangir shuffled to the limit of his chains, and then strained slowly against them; he put his mighty strength into the task, and presently Hussein was awakened by the clear, sharp sound of snapping iron. The noise was not enough to alarm anyone, so none saw the elephant slip away from the lines like a grey shadow, moving without a sound.

Hussein lay still for a moment, somewhat confused. Then he felt Jehangir moving under him, and he sat up. The elephant had come out on to the road, and was moving rapidly towards the south, where the thick forests lay within a mile of the road. Jehangir left the road, and went into the deep elephant grass which bordered it; he stopped, and stuffed a bunch of tender leaves into his mouth.

'Turn, Light of my soul,' said Hussein, very frightened, 'turn and go back before they find that you are gone. They will say that I have stolen you.' Jehangir remained motionless. Hussein slipped to the ground and argued with the elephant.

'If they catch me now they will send me to the jail for many years, and I shall die,' he said.

But Jehangir only gurgled, and his eye took on an obstinate gleam. 'Turn back before it is too late,' repeated Hussein.

'I cannot hide you, and they will catch us and put heavy irons upon you.' He stormed, but Jehangir only ate leaves, and rolled his head: he pleaded with the elephant, and wept at his feet, but Jehangir only ate wild sugar cane and stood upon three legs to rest the fourth.

At length Hussein stood speechless, and Jehangir reached

out his trunk and putting his mahout up on his back again he set off towards the forest.

Then the mahout gave in, and guided the elephant on to a path which led more straightly to the deep woods. He urged Jehangir to his full speed, a peculiar loping shuffle, which took them along at a great speed; for, as he told the elephant, they would have to go far before dawn in order to have a chance of getting clear away. With his tireless gait the elephant gained the virgin forest before the moon had set, and by dawn they were so far away from the camp that Hussein felt safe; nevertheless they kept on until noon, when they rested by a river.

Hussein lay on the warm sand and thought out a plan. He decided to lie hid until the hue and cry died down, and then to go as far south as possible, keeping away from the towns; then he thought that he would travel slowly about the country, hiring Jehangir and himself to clear away trees and to do work for which a well-guided elephant is essential. He had encountered men who owned an elephant and who travelled like this, so his appearance would give rise to no suspicion.

He decided that he would do this until he had amassed sufficient money to buy land and to settle down with Jehangir who would be able to do the work of many bullocks without feeling it.

Hussein lived in the forest with Jehangir for some weeks before he thought it safe to move up the river to where he knew the Grand Trunk Road crossed it on a bridge.

He altered Jehangir's appearance as much as possible, scrubbing off the Government broad arrow, and paring away the Government number from the nail of his right fore-foot; he also took the silver bands from the elephant's tusks and put them on his wrists as bracelets to make himself look respectably wealthy.

They made their way slowly up the river until they came to the road, which Hussein meant to cross so as to avoid observation, but the first thing they met as they crossed an unfrequented stretch was a man on a Goverment elephant.

This was the same man who had caused Hussein to be beaten some time before. They recognized one another at once, the man bawled, 'Stop thief,' and urged his elephant forward, beating with his heavy ankus.

Hussein leaned forward and spoke to Jehangir, who burst into a tremendous gallop. There was open country the other side of the road thinly interspersed with trees. Jehangir charged across the road and thundered away over the plain. The man set his elephant in pursuit, and the two rushed furiously away towards the west.

Very soon Hussein saw that Jehangir was losing ground, so he pulled up, and the two elephants faced one another.

Suddenly they both charged, and met head-on with a thud that shook the ground. Forehead to forehead they pushed furiously, each trying to force the other backwards.

The two mahouts hurled abuse at one another as their mounts strove with all their great strength.

His opponent was gaining a little, being somewhat heavier, so Jehangir, getting a foothold in the loose soil made an immense effort, so great that his fore-feet left the ground and he leaned with all his weight on his enemy, who began sliding slowly backwards, his feet slipping in the dust.

At the same moment Hussein leapt across on to the other elephant's neck, and seizing the mahout, he cast him down.

In another second Jehangir had defeated his opponent, thrusting him backwards and sideways; very quickly Jehangir backed, and then charged, ramming the other elephant in the side. He went over with a crash right on top of his mahout, who was struggling on the ground. Hussein had time to leap clear, and immediately he ran to Jehangir to stop him battering the other elephant to death. Jehangir obeyed at once, and Hussein, mounting on to his neck, guided him back into the forest.

Having concealed him in a clump of bamboos and forbidden him to move, Hussein went back to the dead mahout. There was nothing to be done for him; the falling elephant had killed him instantly, and in a panic had run back to his elephant lines.

Presently the people who saw him return without his mahout sent out a search party, who found the body, and Hussein, coming up as if he knew nothing about it, learnt that the man had been trampled to death by his own elephant, which he was known to have treated cruelly.

Nobody recognized Hussein or suspected him even when he appeared riding on Jehangir; it was a district in which he had never been before, and his story was accepted without the slightest question.

Once he was safely away in the south Hussein carried out the rest of his plan, and in time he bought three fields and a small house in which he lived very happily, although he was hard put to it to find a shelter for Jehangir in the rains.

JELLALUDIN

XII

Jellaludin

Hussein, before he had acquired his elephant, had been a snake-charmer, and at that time he had possessed a mongoose.

Jellaludin, as the mongoose was called, on account of his whiskers, was quite good enough for Hussein's purposes. Hussein became quite attached to Jellaludin, for the mongoose was very intelligent, even if he was somewhat fat and lazy.

In time Jellaludin grew accustomed to Hussein's three tame cobras, all of whom had their fangs drawn, and although the sight of a strange snake made the fur rise all along his back, he quite liked the three lazy old snakes who lived in Hussein's flat-bottomed basket.

During the heat of the summer it was Hussein's custom to follow the white people up to the hill stations, for they always paid well if they were amused.

He did not confine himself to giving performances with his snakes, however; he also used his snake-charming powers to free houses from snakes. He did it in this way: first he would make the acquaintance of some tradesmen who knew all about the white people, and from them Hussein would find out which of the sahibs had wives; then he would go to the houses of these sahibs and bribe the *khansamah* to let him give a performance in the compound.

After the performance he would announce that he felt the presence of snakes in the house itself, and if this made a suitable impression upon the white people, he would offer to come back in the evening to catch the snakes – for a modest fee, of course.

Then he would go round to the servants' quarters, and get them, with a promise of commission, to secrete his tame snakes in the house. One – the largest – he always had put in the bedroom, another in the bathroom, and a third in any conveniently dramatic place. Towards sundown he would return, looking important, with a sack for the snakes, his flute, and Jellaludin.

In the house he would go from room to room, sniffing; when he came to the bedroom he would assure the mem-sahib that there was a cobra in the room, then he would squat down on the floor and, having produced Jellaludin from a fold inside his voluminous robes, he would play on his squeaky, globular flute, while the mongoose went round and round the walls, sniffing.

When he felt that the tension had reached its climax, Hussein would change his tune, and the well-trained cobra would glide out from beneath the pillow and swell out its hood, hissing furiously. Then Jellaludin, who knew his part quite as well, would dart at the snake and leap at its head; before any harm could be done, however, Hussein would rush at the cobra, and bundle it into his sack.

After he had gone from room to room, and collected his snakes, he could be practically certain of about four rupees from the grateful white people, and more if they were newcomers, but at least half of his reward had to go in commissions to the servants.

When there was a child in the house, however, he could always be sure of at least ten rupees, for if he had heard that there was a child, he would borrow trained snakes from any of the fakirs of his acquaintance who possessed them, so that he could produce as many as ten of the reptiles from all around the child's cot before its parents' horrified eyes. This was particularly well paid, though of course the commissions to the servants and the fakirs were higher.

The only thing that sometimes put Hussein off his stroke on such occasions was Jellaludin, who, though he did his best, could not always distinguish between the strange tame snakes and snakes that he was really supposed to kill; and then towards the end of the performance, when he had apparently slain nearly a dozen snakes to the accompaniment of furious leaping in the air, he became rather tired, owing to his fatness, and he was not quite so spectacular as Hussein might have wished, but on the whole things went off very satisfactorily.

Now it came to Hussein's ears when he was in Simla that the wife of the District Magistrate of Jullundur was known to be extremely fearful of snakes, and that her husband was very wealthy. This he heard from a sunyassi who had borrowed Jellaludin for a day; the mendicant had also remarked that the magistrate had two young children.

So Hussein, who had got all that could be expected in one season from the white people in Simla, packed up his snakes, his flute, and his few other belongings in an ancient piece of cloth, and, calling Jellaludin from under the thatch of the roof, he set off south.

After a certain time had passed he came to Jullundur, where he sought out one of his friends, a sadhu who dealt in curses of all kinds.

From the sadhu Hussein borrowed no less than nine assorted serpents, ranging from a small but venomous *krait* to an immense hamadryad cobra. They were all well trained, and Hussein spent a whole day in getting Jellaludin used to them.

All his usual preliminaries went well, and one evening a week after his arrival in Jullundur he began to extract snakes from the magistrate's house.

He had various less spectacular snakes scattered in the usual places, but he had at least six concealed about the magistrate's children's nursery.

He came to this room last of all, and when he had played his flute for a little while the snakes began to come out into the open. One flopped down from a tear in the ceiling cloth, two more came from a rat hole in a corner, and the great hamadryad came from under one of the cots.

At first everything went well, and Hussein had most of the snakes in his sack before he noticed that Jellaludin was not doing his part at all well, indeed he looked quite languid.

The mongoose was so slow in dealing with the big cobra that before Hussein could very well say that Jellaludin had finished with it, another snake came out, and the white people, who were looking on, became most uneasy.

Hussein became rather flurried, and before he had dealt with it, the sixth snake came from the hole in the wall where the punkah came through. The white man leapt for his riding crop, and he killed the unfortunate snake by breaking its back. Hurriedly bundling the other two into his sack, Hussein cursed the magistrate bitterly in Urdu.

Unhappily for the snake-charmer, the magistrate knew the tongue perfectly, and replied in the same language; then he clapped his hands to call the servants, whom he told to throw Hussein out of the house.

This was done, and in the doing two of the snakes were hurt. The dead snake was the small blue *krait* belonging to the sadhu; it was said to be valuable on account of the various tricks it could perform. When the sadhu heard of its death, and saw two of his other snakes wounded, he cursed Hussein root and branch; and he also exacted ten rupees by way of compensation.

Hussein blamed Jellaludin bitterly, for if he had done what he had to do quickly, instead of being lazy, everything would have been well, and the white man would have given him at least fifteen rupees, and saying this, Hussein cuffed the mongoose repeatedly, threatening to drown him in a well.

Jellaludin felt the disgrace keenly and went off his feed, with the result that he grew quite thin.

Fortunately Hussein had saved his own three cobras, so he was able to keep going by performing with them, although the sadhu had taken all his resources.

He left Jullundur as soon as possible, and turned up, after wandering for some time, at Benares, where he hoped to pick up some information from the host of mendicants and wandering priests who thronged the holy city.

For two days he sat before the great temple of Kali, speaking with the crowds of assorted fakirs who resorted to it.

On the third day he saw an old friend of his, a sunyassi who cast horoscopes, and from him Hussein learnt that a group of English tourists would be staying at the house of the political officer in one of the small principalities, and that the rajah was going to give them a feast, as they were quite distinguished politicians.

Hussein knew that all kinds of entertainers would be wanted, so he went towards Kapilavatthu, the rajah's capital. On the way he encountered a company of dancers who were going to the same place, so he travelled with them, arriving at Kapilavatthu in a week.

After the feast Hussein gave a performance with his snakes which went off quite well. On the next day he presented himself at the political officer's house, having had ten trained snakes, which he had borrowed, placed in strategic points, and he announced that he would free the house from the snakes which he felt sure were in it.

The Resident had seen it done before, and he had a shrewd idea of how it was worked, but he thought that it would impress his guests, and might even stop the distinguished politicians talking for a little while, so Hussein was admitted.

First he produced snakes from the ceiling cloth – it was

very striking to see a fat, writhing cobra wriggling out of the ceiling — and then he piped them out from underneath the white peoples' beds. After that he went to the large, white tiled bathroom, which was the joy of the Resident's heart, where he had his last two snakes concealed.

Hussein, having put them back into his sack, was beginning to make his preparations for departure, when he saw, to his horror, another snake creeping out of the drain-pipe.

It was a great hamadryad cobra, one of the most venomous of snakes. In the hope that it would go back when it saw the people, Hussein kept on piping with his flute; but the cobra came on, and by the time it was half-way out, Jellaludin, who had been sniffing about on the other side of the room, saw it, and darted forward.

Hussein was very much afraid lest Jellaludin should take it for one of the trained snakes, and only nip it gently in the neck, for if it did, the mongoose would undoubtedly be bitten, and if he could not find a certain herb to eat in time, he would certainly die.

This herb is only known to the mongooses, who run to find it if ever they get bitten in a fight with a snake, and when they eat it, it counteracts the poison, and they take no harm.

As soon as Jellaludin got near the snake, he realized that something was wrong, and he danced round on his toes, keeping at a safe distance.

The big cobra came fully out of the drain-pipe, and coiled itself so as to be ready to strike.

The mongoose darted round and round it, drawing slightly nearer. Suddenly the hamadryad struck, missing

Jellaludin by an inch. It smacked against the white tiles with a sound of a cracked whip, and the mongoose sprang back out of reach.

Hussein could not go to his help, as the cobra would have bitten him, and he would have died within an hour.

The snake recoiled itself, and Jellaludin began going round it again. It turned steadily, watching for a chance to strike. It thought it saw an opportunity, but the mongoose was out of reach, and as the snake faltered for a split second, Jellaludin leapt at its head. He got a grip on its neck just below the hood – too low down – and the cobra, twisting its head managed to bite Jellaludin twice before its spine was broken.

Without pausing for a moment Jellaludin dropped the inert body, and leapt out of the open window into the garden; he had no time to waste if he was to save his life.

He saw a patch of neglected grass, and darted into it, sniffing eagerly. Soon he found that which he sought, and having eaten the bitter herb, he looked for water.

In the house the white man crushed the cobra's head under the heel of his boot, and Hussein put the body into a bag, for if Jellaludin was still alive he would love the cobra as a meal.

Barely waiting for his money, Hussein hurried out of the house.

He found the mongoose sitting on the gravel drive, licking the bites. Seeing Hussein he trotted up and jumped on to his shoulder, from whence he crept into the inside pocket in which he always travelled.

Then Hussein knew that all was well, for if the mongoose

had been going to die, he would have known it, and crept away to some quiet, dark place to die in peace.

When they reached the house in which he was staying, Hussein produced the dead cobra from the bag, and laid it in a quiet corner.

Jellaludin began at the tail.